Shannon
the Ocean
Fairy

Special thanks to
Narinder Dhami

ISBN 978-0-545-10576-7

15 14   13/0
Printed in the U.S.A.   40

First Scholastic Printing, April 2009

Shannon
the Ocean
Fairy

by Daisy Meadows

SCHOLASTIC INC.

New York   Toronto   London   Auckland
Sydney   Mexico City   New Delhi   Hong Kong

The
Fairyland
Palace

Hawaiian Island

Surfing Waves

Dolphins

← Coral Reef

Baby Seahorses

The Dawn
Pearl

To the palace we will go,
Because my spell will make it so.
Enchanted pearls I plan to take.
Leaving chaos in my wake!

Tides will rise to flood both worlds,
While my goblins have the pearls.
So, goblins, keep them safe for me,
Hidden deep beneath the sea.

Find the hidden letters in the starfish throughout this book. Unscramble all 7 letters to spell a special ocean word!

Contents

Party in Fairyland

"Race you to that tidepool, Kirsty!" Rachel Walker yelled to her best friend, Kirsty Tate.

"You're on!" Kirsty replied.

Laughing, the two girls ran across the beach. Rachel reached the pool first, but Kirsty was right behind her.

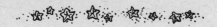

"Your gran is lucky to live in Leamouth!" Rachel panted, gazing around the sandy bay. "It's so pretty."

Kirsty nodded. Leamouth was a little fishing village with winding streets and a harbor filled with boats. Kirsty's gran lived in a cottage on the cliff, near the beach.

"I always have fun here," said Kirsty. "I'm glad you could come this time, too."

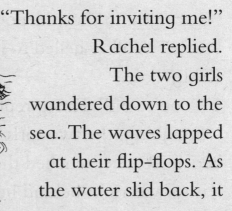

"Thanks for inviting me!" Rachel replied. The two girls wandered down to the sea. The waves lapped at their flip-flops. As the water slid back, it

left a large seashell
on the sand right
in front of them.
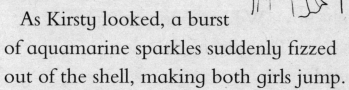
Rachel picked it
up. "It's beautiful,"
she said.

As Kirsty looked, a burst
of aquamarine sparkles suddenly fizzed
out of the shell, making both girls jump.

Kirsty gasped. "Fairy magic!"

The girls glanced at each other, eyes
wide with excitement. Their friendship
with the fairies was a very special secret.

Soft music and the faint tinkle of
bells floated out of the shell. Quickly,
Rachel held it up so she and Kirsty could
listen.

"Hello, girls," said a small voice.

Rachel grinned at Kirsty. "It's the fairy queen!" she exclaimed.

"We'd like to invite you to a special beach party — a luau — to celebrate summer," the queen said. "If you'd like to come, just place the shell on the sand right now. We hope you can join us. . . ." The queen's voice faded away.

With a quick
glance around to
make sure nobody was
watching, Rachel placed
the seashell on the sand.
Immediately, a dazzling rainbow
sprang from the shell. Its colors
were bright in the sunshine.
"Let's go, Kirsty!" Rachel whispered.
Kirsty nodded, and the girls
stepped onto the rainbow. As soon as
they did, they were whisked away
in a whirl of fairy magic.
When the sparkles vanished, the girls
had been magically transformed into
fairies. They were in Fairyland, standing
on a beautiful sandy beach next to a

glittering turquoise sea. The beach was crowded with fairies enjoying the luau.

As the girls stepped away from the rainbow, their fairy friends rushed to greet them, including King Oberon and Queen Titania.

"We're so glad you could come, girls," the king said kindly.

"A party wouldn't be the same without you," the queen added.

"Thank you for inviting us," Rachel and Kirsty chorused. "Come and dance!" called Jade the Disco Fairy. Laughing, Rachel and Kirsty joined Jade. Meanwhile, they could see another fairy conducting the musicians, and other fairies cooking food on a barbecue.

"The tide's coming in," Rachel remarked to Jade as the waves crept further up the beach. "Will the party be over soon?"

Jade shook her head. "No, we'll be fine as long as we stay above Party

Rock," she replied, pointing to a large boulder nearby. "But Shannon the Ocean Fairy can explain it better than I can." A nearby fairy turned and smiled at the girls. She wore a peach-colored skirt, a top made of aqua ribbons, and a glittering starfish clip in her hair.

"Hi, girls," Shannon greeted them. "Jade's right. The sea never comes past Party Rock, so we can enjoy the party all day long!"

"Great!" Rachel said happily.

A little while later, the girls were still having fun dancing with their fairy

friends when the music suddenly stopped. Everyone turned to see what had happened.

"Listen, please," called Shannon the Ocean Fairy. "I'm afraid that the sea is coming in too far!"

She pointed her wand at Party Rock and everyone gasped in surprise. The water was splashing around the base of the rock, and the level was still rising!

"The water never comes in this far," Shannon declared anxiously. "Something's wrong!"

High Tide

King Oberon frowned. "Maybe Jack Frost is up to no good again," he said.

Queen Titania nodded and turned to Rachel and Kirsty. "Girls, would you come back to the palace with us?" she asked. "You might be able to help."

"Of course we will," Kirsty and Rachel replied together. Whenever Jack Frost

and his goblins caused trouble in
Fairyland, the girls were happy to help
their fairy friends!

"I'll explore my underwater world and
see if I can find out why the sea is
rising," Shannon said, diving gracefully
into the ocean.

Quickly, the other
fairies began to leave the
beach. Meanwhile,
the king and queen led
Rachel and Kirsty back to
the Fairyland palace.

"We'll go to the Royal Observatory,"
King Oberon said. "It's at the top of the
tallest tower. The roof slides back so
that our telescopes can look out on the
night sky."

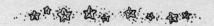

"And Cedric, our Royal Astronomer, guards the enchanted pearls there," Queen Titania said as they climbed the spiral staircase. "The pearls are magical. They're very important in Fairyland — and in your world, too."

"Why?" Kirsty asked.

"The pink Dawn Pearl makes sure that dawn comes each morning so the day can begin," the queen explained. "It also affects the levels of water in the oceans."

"The silver Twilight Pearl makes sure that night falls every evening," the king added. "And the final pearl is the creamy-white Moon Pearl. It controls the flow of water through the oceans and the size of the waves." He sighed. "I

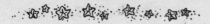

think that something is wrong
with the Dawn Pearl,
and that's why the
sea is coming
in so far."

Rachel and
Kirsty followed
the king and
queen into the
observatory.
The room was
painted white,
but the sliding
roof was deep
blue, like the night
sky. There were
large golden telescopes
around the room, and star
charts hung on the walls.

14

"Cedric!" Queen Titania exclaimed, and the girls suddenly noticed a frog footman sitting on the floor, looking dazed. He was wrapped in a long velvet cloak embroidered with moons and stars. "What happened?" asked the queen, hurrying over to him. "Are you all right?" Cedric looked very upset. He pointed to a crystal box that was lying open on the floor. "Jack Frost and his goblins have stolen the enchanted pearls!" he told the queen sadly. "What?" King Oberon exclaimed.

"Jack Frost again!"
Kirsty whispered to Rachel.
"Let's see exactly what
happened," said Queen
Titania, pointing her
wand upward.

As magic from the queen's wand
streamed across the ceiling, images began
to appear. There was Cedric, studying a
large chart, when a blast of wind
suddenly swept the door open. Jack Frost
and a group of goblins burst in!

Shocked, Cedric leapt to his feet, but
Jack Frost pointed his wand at him. An
icy breeze shot toward the footman,
whirling his cloak around him and tying
him up in knots.

"Help!" Cedric cried, as a fold of the
cloak wrapped itself around his head.

Jack Frost smirked.
"Quick! Get the
enchanted pearls!" he
shouted to his gang of
goblins.

While Cedric
struggled with his
cloak, three goblins
rushed over to the
crystal box. They
flung the lid back and
grabbed the large,
gleaming pearls: one
pink, one white, and

one silver. Throwing the box carelessly to the floor, the goblins held the pearls up triumphantly.

Jack Frost looked very pleased. "This serves those horrible fairies right!" he cried. "The king and queen banned me from the luau because I haven't been behaving myself. Well, without the enchanted pearls, their beach party will be a washout!"

He laughed spitefully. "There's going to be chaos in the fairy and

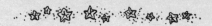

human worlds without these pearls.
Time and tides, daybreak and
nightfall — everything will
be disrupted!"

"Great idea, boss!"
said one of the
goblins. "Where
should we hide
the pearls?"

"The fairies
always find the
magic objects we
steal. I'm fed up with
it!" Jack Frost said.
"This time, we will hide
the pearls in the human world — but
underwater!"

The goblins looked terrified. "But we
can't breathe underwater," they moaned.

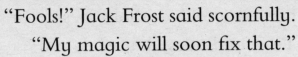

"Fools!" Jack Frost said scornfully. "My magic will soon fix that." He pointed his wand at the goblins and a stream of large, icy bubbles flew from it. Each bubble floated down over one of the goblins' heads like an old-fashioned diving helmet.

"Now you can breathe underwater," Jack Frost said. "And these," he went on, aiming his wand at the goblins' big green feet, "will make you super-speedy swimmers."

A burst of frosty sparkles swirled around the goblins' feet. Suddenly, they were all wearing huge black flippers!

Jack Frost looked sternly at the goblins. "Now keep those enchanted pearls safe,

or you'll have me to answer to!" With
another wave of his wand, a freezing
wind sprang up and swept the goblins
straight out of the window with the
enchanted pearls.

Underwater World

"I'm so sorry," Cedric said, burying his head in his hands as the pictures faded away.

"It's not your fault, Cedric," Queen Titania said gently.

"We have to tell Shannon what happened," King Oberon declared, waving his wand.

Seconds later, Shannon fluttered into the observatory. "Your Majesties," she cried, "my underwater world is in chaos! The tides are all wrong, and it's upsetting the sea creatures."

"That's not surprising," King Oberon said grimly. "Jack Frost has stolen the three enchanted pearls. He sent his goblins to hide them in the ocean in the human world."

Shannon looked horrified. "But that's going to affect the seas, daytime, and nighttime in the human world *and* in Fairyland!" she said.

The queen nodded. "It's up to you, Shannon," she said. "Do you think you can get the pearls back?"

"I'll do my best," Shannon replied.

"We'll help," Rachel said eagerly. "Right, Kirsty?"

Kirsty agreed. "Of course. Except that we can't breathe underwater."

Shannon grinned. "That's no problem, girls!"

She raised her wand, and the girls saw two shiny bubbles stream toward them. They felt the bubbles settle over their heads, and heard a *POP* as the bubbles disappeared.

"Now you can breathe underwater," Shannon announced. "Let's go. There isn't a moment to lose!"

"Good luck," the queen called as Shannon raised her wand again. "And remember, the enchanted pearls will be much bigger in the human world!"

As magic sparkles from Shannon's wand sprinkled down around them, Rachel and Kirsty shut their eyes.

"Welcome to my underwater world," Shannon said a moment later.

The girls opened their eyes. To their amazement, they were standing on a sandy golden seabed, surrounded by huge shells and pink coral.

"We're under the sea!" Kirsty cried, clapping her hand to her mouth in astonishment. She was breathing and talking normally, as if she was on land! The water didn't even feel wet.

"It's magical!" Rachel agreed, staring as a large fish with an amazing striped mane swam by.

"That's a lionfish,"
Shannon explained. Then
she turned her head to one
side, listening carefully.
The girls listened, too. They
could hear a strange barking sound,
which gradually got louder and louder.

"Ah, now here are some friends who
will help us find the goblins!" Shannon
exclaimed happily. A moment later, a
pack of sea lions came racing through
the water, their sleek black bodies
twisting and turning.

"Hello!" Shannon called.

The girls watched, enchanted, as the
sea lions bounced playfully around
them, chattering and barking loudly.
They reminded Rachel of a pack of
friendly dogs.

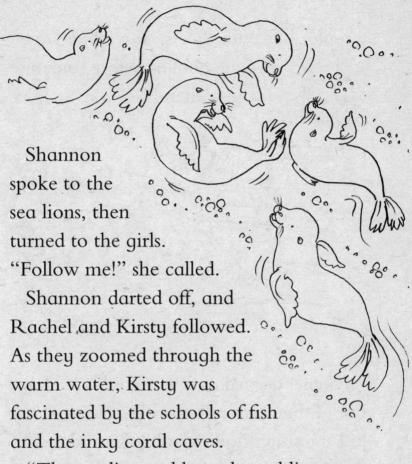

Shannon
spoke to the
sea lions, then
turned to the girls.
"Follow me!" she called.

Shannon darted off, and
Rachel and Kirsty followed.
As they zoomed through the
warm water, Kirsty was
fascinated by the schools of fish
and the inky coral caves.

"The sea lions told me the goblins are
near this shipwreck site," Shannon said,
pointing ahead at the remains of an old
Spanish ship on the sea floor. "It's a very

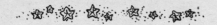

popular place for divers, so we have to
find the goblins before someone
spots them!"

Rachel gasped as a woman loomed up
out of the sand in front of her. "Oh, it's
just the ship's figurehead!" she said,
touching the peeling paint.

Just then, Kirsty spotted a glint of gold
on the seabed. "That's a gold coin!" she
said excitedly, pointing. "Look how

brightly it's shining. There's a lot of light around here."

"I know why," Shannon replied. "This isn't normal sunlight. It's the magical light of the Dawn Pearl!"

"Shh!" Rachel hissed suddenly, putting her finger to her lips. "I hear goblin voices!"

Shannon, Rachel, and Kirsty quickly swam behind a nearby rock and peeked out cautiously. A moment later, three goblins came swimming toward them — and one was carrying the Dawn Pearl!

A Treasure Trail

Rachel and Kirsty caught their breath as they gazed at the pearl. It was a beautiful pink color, and it shone with a dazzling brightness that filled the ocean with light.

Shannon and the girls watched as the goblins suddenly shot forward. Their magic flippers propelled them quickly through the water.

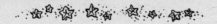

"They're very fast swimmers with those flippers," Shannon whispered. "We won't be able to catch up if we have to chase them!"

The goblins began to swim around the wreck of the Spanish ship, holding the pearl out in front of them.

"They're using the pearl like a flashlight!" Shannon frowned. "I hope none of the human divers around here spot the light."

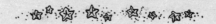

"The goblins are looking for something," whispered Kirsty.

"There's no treasure here!" the biggest goblin exclaimed in disgust. "Let's look somewhere else."

The goblins moved away from the ship and swam along the seabed. Shannon and the girls followed, staying hidden.

"Look, a treasure chest!" The smallest goblin squealed, pointing at a tarnished silver chest, half-buried in the sand. He swam down and heaved the lid open. Then he shrieked in fear as a group of brightly colored fish swam out!

The other goblins roared with laughter. Shannon grinned too,

but her face fell quickly. "Oh, no!" she cried. "Girls, this is terrible!"

Rachel and Kirsty looked around, confused.

"Do you see that opening in the rocks over there?" Shannon whispered, pointing at a narrow gap in a nearby rock wall.

The opening was surrounded by vibrant blue-and-green seaweed and amazingly bright pink sea anemones.

"That's the entrance to the Mermaid Kingdom," Shannon went on.

"You mean, mermaids are real?" Rachel gasped.

"Yes, but they're very secretive," Shannon explained. "They're scared of being discovered by humans and having their kingdom revealed.

Imagine what a mess that would be!"

Rachel and Kirsty gazed in wonder at the narrow rocky pass. It was lit brightly by the Dawn Pearl.

"If any divers come along now, they'll spot the goblins — and maybe find the Mermaid Kingdom, too!" Shannon said anxiously.

Kirsty glanced at the goblins. Suddenly an idea popped into her head. "Maybe we can lure the goblins away with some treasure!" she exclaimed. "If you could

use your magic to make some gold coins,
Shannon, we could lay a trail for the
goblins to follow."

"I can do that," Shannon agreed. "The
magic coins won't last forever, but they
should stay long enough to fool the silly
goblins."

"We could trap them in one of those
coral caves we saw on the way here,"
Kirsty went on.

"Good idea," Rachel said eagerly. "If the goblins are trapped, maybe we can get the Dawn Pearl back."

"And I know just how we can trap them!" Shannon declared eagerly. "I'll be back in a minute, girls."

With that, she swam away, returning quickly. "I've asked some friends for help," she explained, winking at the girls. "Now, let me use my magic to make a trail of gold!"

Shannon waved her wand. The girls saw a trail of shiny coins appear in the

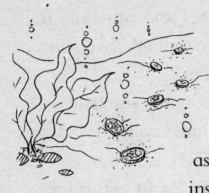

sand, leading into a nearby coral cave. "I hope the goblins spot them," Shannon whispered as the three friends hid inside the Spanish ship.

The goblins were still swinging the Dawn Pearl through the water, searching for treasure. Suddenly, one of the goblins gave a shriek of triumph as he spotted a gold coin glinting in the sand.

"Treasure!" he yelled, scooping it up.

Shannon and the girls grinned at each other.

"I see another one!" the biggest goblin shouted, dashing forward to grab a second coin.

Shannon, Rachel, and Kirsty swam silently after the excited goblins as they picked up the gold coins, one by one. The goblins paused outside the cave, and Kirsty held her breath.

Would they go in?

In the Coral Cave

To Kirsty's relief, the goblins hurried inside the coral cave.

"Let's go!" Shannon whispered. She and the girls swam over to the mouth of the cave. Inside, the goblins were scrambling around on the sandy floor, looking for more coins.

Shannon cleared her throat loudly, and the goblins yelped with surprise.

"Please give me the Dawn Pearl," Shannon said politely.

"No way!" the goblins scoffed.

"We're not letting you leave until you do," Rachel told them.

"You silly little fairies can't stop us!" the biggest goblin declared, moving toward the girls. His friends followed.

Just as the girls were wondering what to do, they heard a snapping sound. Looking down, they saw an army of

lobsters scuttling into the cave and snapping at the goblins' ankles with their claws. The goblins screeched and backed away!

"We can't stop you," Shannon said, "but my lobster friends can. They'll snap at your ears — and noses, too — if you don't give back the Dawn Pearl." The goblins looked annoyed for a minute, but they couldn't help squealing in fear when the lobsters scuttled toward them again. "OK," the biggest

goblin muttered.
"It's yours!"

The goblins
tossed the
Dawn Pearl
across the cave,
and Shannon,
Rachel, and Kirsty
caught it between them.

"Thank you," Shannon called. "And
thank you to my lobster friends, too."

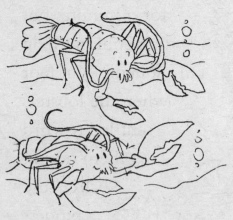

She waved her
wand. A burst of
fairy dust swept
Rachel and
Kirsty out of
the water in
an instant!

Blinking as the magic dust cleared, the girls realized that they were back on the beach in Leamouth.

"We're not even wet," Kirsty said, looking down at her dry clothes.

"That's fairy magic!" Shannon laughed. She tapped the tip of her wand on the Dawn Pearl and it immediately shrank down to Fairyland size. Then

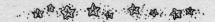

another sparkling shower of fairy dust returned Kirsty and Rachel to their normal sizes again!

"I need to take the Dawn Pearl back to Fairyland now," Shannon said. "Thank you for all your help! We still have a hard task ahead of us. We have to find the two other enchanted pearls!"

Rachel and Kirsty nodded and waved, ready for the challenge. Their fairy friend blew them a kiss, then disappeared with the Dawn Pearl in a whirl of fairy magic.

Trouble at Sea

Contents

At the Pier

"It's another sunny day, Rachel!" said Kirsty. "What should we do?"

It was the morning after their undersea adventure, and the girls were getting ready to go out with Kirsty's gran.

"Anything is fine with me," Rachel replied. She glanced over at Gran, who was cleaning up the kitchen, and lowered

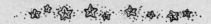

her voice. "Maybe we helped make the day start so bright and sunny by finding the Dawn Pearl."

"Maybe," Kirsty said, nodding. "I hope we get a chance to help Shannon look for the other missing pearls today."

"How about a walk to the pier this morning, girls?" Gran suggested.

"That's a great idea!" Kirsty exclaimed. "There's a fairground at the end of the pier with a roller coaster that goes right out over the water!"

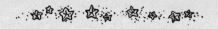

"Ooh, fun!" Rachel said with a grin.

Gran laughed. "Come on, then."

They set off along the water toward the pier.

"Look at that big cruise ship out at sea," Gran remarked, as they walked by the harbor.

Rachel and Kirsty looked out across the water. They could see a huge white ship with black smokestacks in the distance.

"It probably won't be stopping in Leamouth," Gran went on. "Those big ships never dock here."

"Look, Rachel, there's the old lighthouse," Kirsty said, pointing. "There are some really dangerous rocks around the harbor, so the lighthouse was built to guide ships in safely."

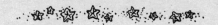

Rachel stared up at the white-and-red-painted lighthouse. It stood on a rocky outcrop at the entrance to the harbor. "Does it still work?" she asked.

Gran shook her head. "No, modern ships have all sorts of high-tech equipment to guide them these days," she replied. "There are plans to turn the lighthouse into an artists' studio."

With that, they kept walking toward the pier at the other end of the beach.

"I bet you girls want to explore," Gran said as they reached the pier. "I'll have a drink in the café and wait for you."

Gran led the way to The Starfish Café and sat down at a table that looked out over the sea.

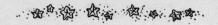

"A pot of tea for one, please," Gran told the waiter.

The man chatted while he wrote the order on his notepad. "See that big cruise ship out there?" he said to Gran and the girls. "It's called the *Seafarer*. They just said on the radio that it's going to dock right here in Leamouth!"

"Really?" Gran asked, looking surprised. "That's unusual."

"Yes, it sounds like the ship is having problems with its navigation systems. It needs to dock as soon as possible," the man explained. "You'll have a perfect

view of it from this table, though it won't
be docking for an hour or so."

"It'll be so cool to see the ship coming
in," Rachel said.

Gran checked her watch. "Well, why
don't you girls go explore, and then
come back to watch the ship dock?" she
suggested. "I'll sit here and read until you
get back," she added, pulling a book out
of her purse.

"Sure — see you later, Gran," said
Kirsty, as she and Rachel walked down
the pier.

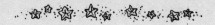

"The sky looks really black over there by the harbor entrance, even though the sun's shining," Rachel noted, pointing out to sea.

Kirsty nodded. "Maybe there's a storm coming," she replied.

The girls walked by a small arcade. Suddenly, the lights on a machine by the entrance started flashing, and a happy tune rang through the air.

Rachel stopped. "*FREE PLAY,*" she read aloud from the little screen.

"Go ahead!" Kirsty urged her friend. "I've tried this kind of game before, but I'm no good at it," Rachel admitted.

The machine was full of stuffed animals in a glass case. A large metal claw hung above them. The claw was operated by a lever and was used to grab the toys. Rachel took hold of the lever and moved the claw downward. It swung around a bit, but Rachel finally managed to grab a fluffy dolphin.

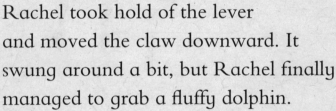

"Go, Rachel!" Kirsty cried, as Rachel carefully moved the dolphin over to the chute and released the metal claw. "You did it!" Kirsty laughed.

Smiling, Rachel pulled back the panel to retrieve her prize. She gasped as a cloud of aquamarine sparkles burst out!

"Hello, girls!" Shannon the Ocean
Fairy cried. "I need your help to find the
Twilight Pearl — and fast!"

Dolphins in the Dark

Rachel and Kirsty were excited to help.

"You'll have to be fairy-size," Shannon said. "Quick, get out of sight."

Rachel and Kirsty ducked behind the machine. One flick of Shannon's wand transformed them into fairies, complete with glittering wings!

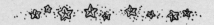

Like before, Shannon created invisible magic bubbles to help the girls breathe underwater.

"Let's go, girls," Shannon said, flying off toward the end of the pier. Rachel and Kirsty zoomed after her.

"Nightfall is already being thrown off in parts of the world because the Twilight Pearl is missing," Shannon explained as they flew. "Last night, darkness didn't fall at the South Pole at all. Luckily, only the penguins noticed!"

"There aren't any people living at the South Pole, are there?" asked Rachel.

"No, there aren't," Shannon replied, "so no humans have noticed the problem yet. But if the Twilight Pearl isn't returned to its usual place soon, there will be nighttime trouble everywhere!"

"Where did the goblins take the Twilight Pearl?" Kirsty asked.

"I think they're underwater somewhere around here," Shannon said, nodding. "It's getting dark near the entrance to Leamouth Harbor. The Twilight Pearl must be nearby!"

"Oh, *that's* why it's so dark!"
Rachel said, as they reached the end
of the pier. "We thought there was
a storm coming."

"Follow me!" Shannon called
then. She flew downward
and plunged into the
sparkling blue sea below.

Rachel and Kirsty
dived beneath the waves,
too. The sun filtered
through the water,
lighting up the
golden seabed
and rippling
fronds of
seaweed. A
school of
silvery fish

flickered past them. The girls grinned in delight. "This way!" Shannon said, darting through the turquoise water. Rachel and Kirsty followed until Shannon stopped and turned to face them. "Look, girls," she said. "Can you see how the color of the sea is changing here?" Rachel and Kirsty looked up ahead. Sure enough, the turquoise color of the water was deepening to a dark indigo.

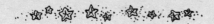

"This is happening because of the Twilight Pearl," Shannon explained. She tapped her wand lightly on her hand, caught a sparkle as it fell, and fixed it to the tip of her wand. It glowed brightly.

"We'll use this to light our way. I just hope the goblins don't see us coming." Shannon swam more slowly this time, with Kirsty and Rachel close behind her. But even though Shannon's glowing wand helped a little, the water around them was growing darker and darker. Kirsty wondered how they were ever going to find the goblins and the Twilight Pearl in the gloom!

Suddenly,
Shannon stopped
again. She tipped
her head to one
side and listened.
"There's someone who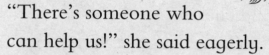
can help us!" she said eagerly.
"Wait here. I'll be back in two shakes of
a fish's tail!" With that, she shot off into
the darkness.

Rachel and Kirsty waited hopefully.
What was their fairy friend up to?

Seconds later, Shannon
returned. "Look who I
found," she announced,
holding up her lighted
wand. Rachel and
Kirsty gasped. Behind
Shannon, they

could see a whole school of
beautiful blue dolphins!

The dolphins were very
friendly. They swam
around Rachel and Kirsty,
squeaking and clicking
in greeting, and
nudging the girls
gently with their
long noses.

"The dolphins
know the oceans
better than anyone
else," Shannon
explained. "They're
going to take us to the
goblins." She waved her
sparkling wand in the air. "Plus,
the dolphins have offered to let us ride

on their backs, so we'll
get there even faster!"
"That's fantastic!"
Rachel exclaimed.
"I've always wanted
to swim with dolphins!"
Kirsty grinned as one
swam over to her and
squeaked, inviting her
to climb aboard. Kirsty
clambered carefully
onto its sleek back, as
Rachel and Shannon
jumped onto their
own dolphins.
"Make sure you hold on tight,"
Shannon called, grabbing onto her
dolphin's fin. "When a dolphin
swims fast, it's *really* fast!"

"I see what you mean!" Kirsty gasped as her dolphin took off like a rocket in the water.

Chattering happily to each other, the rest of the dolphins followed. Rachel and Kirsty hung on tightly as they zipped through the darkening seas.

"This is fun! Woohoo!" Rachel cheered as her dolphin leapt out of the water. It glided through the air in a perfect arc before plunging beneath the waves again.

Soon it was so dark underwater that
Shannon and the girls could hardly even
see each other. Luckily, the dolphins
were still sure of where they were going,
so Rachel and Kirsty didn't feel scared.

Just then, the dolphins began to slow
down. In the darkness, the girls could
hear voices ahead.

"Goblins!" whispered Kirsty.

Grumbling Goblins

The dolphins began to circle the goblins while Shannon, Kirsty, and Rachel stayed very still, listening hard. The goblins sounded scared.

"Oh, I don't like the dark," one whimpered. "Ack! What was that?"

"Maybe it was a sea monster," another moaned. "I can't see."

"Something just swam past me," cried a third. "I think it was an underwater Pogwurzel!"

"HELP!" all the goblins shouted. "WE'RE LOST IN THE DARK!"

Rachel and Kirsty could see Shannon fixing another sparkle to her wand. It fizzed like a firework, lighting up the ocean around them.

The goblins stared in surprise at the circling dolphins.

"It's not a Pogwurzel," one goblin sneered. "It's just some dolphins — and those pesky fairies!"

"Give the Twilight Pearl back, and we'll rescue you from the dark," Shannon offered. "We know you're scared."

"No way!" the biggest goblin scoffed. "We're not scared, and we're not giving back the pearl."

"OK, then we'll leave — and I'll take my light with me," Shannon said firmly.

81

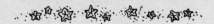

"NO!" all the goblins shrieked at once.
"Please stay," begged the biggest goblin,
looking terrified. "But we can't give the

pearl back."

"Why not?"
asked Rachel.

"Well, it's
just that . . ."
the big goblin
said hesitantly.

"We hid it
somewhere really
safe," another
goblin added.

"And now we can't find it!" said
another, sheepishly.

"But we know it's under a really big
rock," added the largest goblin, trying to
be helpful.

Shannon whipped her
wand through the
water. It briefly lit up
the sea around them.

In that time,
Rachel and Kirsty saw
that the area was *full* of really big rocks!
Suddenly, the booming sound of a
ship's horn echoed overhead. The

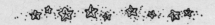

goblins yelped
with fear and
clapped their hands
over their ears.

"I think that must
be the *Seafarer*'s horn,"
said Rachel. "It's coming to dock in
Leamouth because its navigation systems
aren't working."

Shannon turned pale. "The *Seafarer*
won't be able to find its way through the
rocks. It's too dark now that the Twilight
Pearl is missing!" she exclaimed. "It
might crash!"

Rachel and Kirsty glanced
at each other in alarm.
Then Kirsty's gaze
fell on the glowing tip of
Shannon's wand. She

started to get an idea. "The ship would be OK if it had a light to guide it, right?" she pointed out. "Shannon, could you use your magic to get the old lighthouse working again?"

Shannon looked excited. "I think it could," she said. "But we'll have to hurry." She glanced at the goblins. "Stay here and don't make any more trouble!" she told them. "When I get the lighthouse

working, it will be lighter down
here, too."

She jumped off her dolphin, patted its
nose, and then raced up toward the
surface of the water.

Rachel and Kirsty said a quick good-
bye to their dolphins and followed. The
three friends broke through the water
and shot up into the air, then gasped in
amazement.

The Twilight Pearl had made night fall
early. The sky around them was velvety-
black and spangled with stars that
sparkled like diamonds. It was beautiful!

"There's the *Seafarer*," Kirsty shouted,
pointing at the faint silhouette of the ship
near the harbor entrance.

"And look at all those rocks in its
path!" Rachel added.

A Light in the Dark

"To the lighthouse, girls!" Shannon cried. She fluttered off at high speed through the blackness, and the girls zoomed after her.

"How are we going to get inside?" Rachel asked when they reached the locked lighthouse door.

"There's a broken windowpane," Shannon said, pointing upward.

She led the way up to the window and into the dark lighthouse. It smelled dusty and damp as the fairies flew up the spiral staircase to the very top of the tower. Here was the huge lantern, surrounded by mirrors meant to reflect the light out to sea. "Look, the bulb's broken!" Rachel exclaimed, pointing at the lantern.

"The electricity has probably been turned off, anyway," said Kirsty. "The lighthouse hasn't been used in years."

"My fairy magic can fix it," Shannon replied, pointing her wand at the lantern. "But my spell won't last forever. I just hope it's long enough for the *Seafarer* to dock safely."

Rachel and Kirsty watched as a stream of sparkles flew from Shannon's wand and surrounded the lantern.

With lots of loud creaks and groans, the lantern began to turn. Slowly, the broken bulb started to glow, getting brighter and brighter.

"It's lighting up the sea for miles!" Kirsty cheered. "Look, it's showing all the rocks around the mouth of the harbor."

As the three friends watched, the *Seafarer* began to make its way into the harbor. Then Rachel noticed something

strange: every time the lantern's beam
fell on a certain spot in the ocean, she
could see a strange, silvery-gray
shimmer in the water.

"Thank goodness," said Shannon,
once the *Seafarer* had gotten past the
rocks. "Now we'd better see what
those silly goblins are up to."
She flew over to another
window, and Kirsty followed.
But Rachel hesitated, waiting for
the light to fall on the same
patch of water again.

"Shannon, look over there!" Rachel cried, pointing as the sea glittered silvery-gray. "Could the Twilight Pearl be right there, underwater?"

Shannon looked where Rachel was pointing and clapped her hands in delight. "It *is* the Twilight Pearl. I'm sure of it!" she declared.

"Good job, Rachel," Kirsty added.

The three friends flew out of the lighthouse as fast as their wings would take them. They headed straight toward

the glittering patch of water. As they plunged down into the water, the girls were bathed in an eerie silver light that shimmered all around them.

"There it is!" Kirsty exclaimed, spotting the Twilight Pearl beneath a large rock. She gazed at it in wonder. The pearl's silvery glow was truly magical.

But suddenly, to Kirsty's horror, a goblin swam around from the other side of the rock and grabbed the Twilight Pearl!

From Twilight to Sunshine

As Shannon and the girls watched in dismay, all the other goblins appeared.

"Oh no." Rachel groaned. "The beam from the lighthouse helped the goblins find the pearl, too!"

"We'll take that, please," said Kirsty, holding out her hand. But the goblins just laughed.

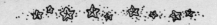

"Go away!" one jeered. "The pearl belongs to us!"

"If you don't give us that pearl right now," Shannon said, looking very serious, "I'll turn the lighthouse off again and leave you here. You know how Pogwurzels love the dark!" She winked at the girls.

The goblins looked panic-stricken. "Take the pearl. Take the pearl!" they yelped, tossing it through the water to the fairies and swimming speedily away.

Laughing, Shannon touched her wand to the Twilight Pearl. It shrank to

fairy-size immediately. She swept it up
into her arms, spinning around in
excitement.

"Everyone in Fairyland will be so

happy to have the
Twilight Pearl
back," she cried.
"But girls, you should
get back to Kirsty's gran
so that you can watch
the *Seafarer* come into
the dock."
The three friends flew
quickly to the deserted end
of the pier. There, Shannon made Kirsty
and Rachel human-size again.

"Now we just have the Moon Pearl
to find," Shannon reminded the girls,
giving them each a quick hug. "See you

again very soon!"
Then she vanished
in a cloud of fairy
dust.

Rachel and
Kirsty hurried back
down the pier. As
they passed the
arcade, Kirsty noticed that the toy
dolphin Rachel had won was still lying
in the chute of the machine.

"Look, here's your dolphin," Kirsty said, handing it to her friend.

"Let's share it," Rachel suggested. "It'll remind us of our amazing underwater adventures!"

Kirsty smiled and the girls ran back to the café, where lots of people had gathered to watch the *Seafarer* approach.

"Ah, there you are, girls," said Gran. "I was worried a storm was on the way, because it was so dark out at sea. But luckily, someone managed to get the old lighthouse working to guide the *Seafarer* in."

Rachel and Kirsty shared a secret smile.

The huge cruise ship was moving slowly into the harbor now. As it did, the darkness began to lift and the sun came out. Everyone clapped and cheered as the ship docked safely.

"Look, the lighthouse is dark again now," Kirsty whispered. "Shannon's fairy magic kept it working just long enough!"

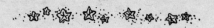

"And the Twilight Pearl is safely back in Fairyland," Rachel added happily. "Now, I wonder where the goblins have hidden the Moon Pearl. . . ."

Pearl Power

Contents

Message in a Bottle

"Oh, dear!" Gran exclaimed as she read the paper the next morning.

"What's the matter, Gran?" asked Kirsty. The girls were getting ready to go down to the beach.

"There are major floods in coastal areas all around the world," Gran explained. "It sounds like the sea is

behaving very strangely. The high tides are coming in much farther than they usually do!"

Rachel and Kirsty glanced at each other in concern. They knew that the Moon Pearl, which controlled the tides, was missing from Fairyland.

"Have fun at the beach, girls, but make sure you're back for lunch," Gran went on. "And keep an eye out for the tides, even though Leamouth doesn't seem too affected right now."

"OK," the girls agreed.

"I wonder if Shannon found out where the goblins are hiding with the Moon

Pearl," Rachel said as they hurried
through the yard and down the cliff steps
to the beach.

"I hope she has," Kirsty replied. "All
those floods sound scary!"

It was still early, so the beach was
deserted. The girls decided to go straight
down to the water. They pulled off their
flip-flops and waded into the cool,
clear sea.

"Isn't it funny to think that we were
actually *under* the sea yesterday?" Kirsty
remarked.

Rachel was about to reply when her eye was caught by a green glass bottle bobbing up and down on the waves. It had a cork in the top. With a rush of excitement, Rachel realized that there was a piece of paper inside.

"Kirsty, look at this," she called, grabbing the bottle as it floated by her. "It's a message in a bottle." Kirsty waded over and peered through the glass at the piece of paper. "It says *Open me!*" she read aloud.

Rachel smiled broadly. "Let's see what happens," she said, pulling out the cork. Immediately, a sparkling mist of turquoise dust burst out of the bottle — and so did Shannon the Ocean Fairy!

Flooding in Fairyland

"Girls, I need your help!" Shannon declared, looking pale. "Fairyland is flooding fast!"

"Oh, no!" Rachel exclaimed.

"Is everyone safe?" Kirsty asked.

Shannon shook her head. "The toadstool houses are all flooding," she explained. "Fairyland is in chaos!"

"How can
we help?"
asked Rachel.
"We need to find
the Moon Pearl
right away," Shannon replied. "And I
think I know where the goblins who
have it are hiding."

"Where?" asked Rachel.

"Hawaii!" Shannon told her.

"Hawaii?" Kirsty repeated, amazed.
"How are we going to get *there*?"

"With fairy magic, of course!"
Shannon laughed. She quickly waved
her wand and turned the girls into
sparkling fairies. Once she had created
some magic bubbles so the girls could
breathe underwater, they were
ready to go.

"Follow me," Shannon said, diving neatly into the waves.

Kirsty and Rachel did the same.

"Now, stay very close," Shannon instructed, linking arms with the girls and waving her wand again.

Rachel and Kirsty let out a gasp as they were swept off their feet at top speed. A magic current carried the three friends through the water. They went so fast that their hair streamed out behind them!

The girls couldn't see anything except for the swirls of rainbow-colored bubbles along the magical stream.

A few minutes later, Rachel and Kirsty felt themselves slowing down.

"That was like a super-fast roller coaster ride!" Rachel exclaimed.

Kirsty nodded. "The water feels much warmer here," she said.

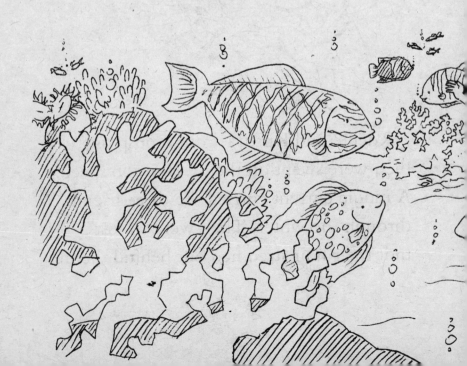

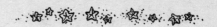

"That's because we're in Hawaii!"
Shannon declared. "See the coral reef?"

Rachel and Kirsty gazed around. The
sea was a clear sapphire-blue. All kinds
of colorful tropical fish were weaving
their way through the reef of pink, red,
and white coral. The sun was shining
through the water, creating pretty
patterns on the sandy seabed.

"Let's go and see what the goblins are up to," Shannon said with a grin. "I think they're up here." She zoomed to the surface, and the girls followed.

Peeking out of the water, Rachel and Kirsty saw a beautiful island with palm trees and a golden, sandy beach.

"Listen," Shannon whispered.

Rachel and Kirsty suddenly realized
that they could hear shouts and whoops
of glee. They turned and saw a big,
rolling wave making its way toward the
beach. And riding on top of the wave, on
brightly colored surfboards, was a group
of giggling goblins!

Weird Waves

Rachel, Kirsty, and Shannon had to muffle their laughter as they watched the goblins surfing. The goblins all had garlands of flowers around their necks. Some were even wearing flowery Hawaiian shirts or long grass skirts — in the water!

"They look so funny!" Rachel giggled.

"But aren't they supposed to be in hiding with the Moon Pearl?"

"I think they've forgotten about that," Shannon replied. "They're having too much fun!"

"These waves are gigantic," Kirsty remarked as another huge wall of water headed toward the beach. "They're perfect for surfing."

Shannon nodded. "Yes, that's what Hawaii's famous for," she said. "But these waves are even bigger than usual!"

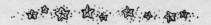

She frowned. "I think the goblins are using the Moon Pearl to make the waves bigger. To do that, they must have the Moon Pearl underwater and close by."

"Let's start searching!" Kirsty said eagerly.

As Rachel and Kirsty looked around for any sign of the Moon Pearl, they suddenly spotted a group of bright blue seahorses bobbing through the water toward them.

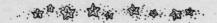

The tiny seahorses swam right up to Shannon and started talking to her in bubbly, high-pitched voices! The girls looked on in awe.

"Aren't they cute?" Kirsty said. "I wonder what they're saying."

Shannon grinned and waved her wand. Rachel and Kirsty suddenly found that

they could understand
the seahorses perfectly!
"Hello, Shannon," the
little seahorses chorused.
"Hello, girls."
"We're very pleased to
meet you," said one.

"Yes, very pleased to meet you," the
others repeated.

Rachel and Kirsty were enchanted.
"We're very pleased to meet you, too,"
they replied.

"These baby seahorses are friends of mine," Shannon explained. "I've known them ever since they were born."

"Yes, ever since we were born!" the seahorses cried in agreement.

"Ever since we were born!" squeaked another one, a little bit behind his friends.

"We're looking for the Moon Pearl," Shannon told them. "Have you seen it?"

The seahorses bounced up and down in the water, looking very

excited. "We think so! We think so!"
they all yelled in their tiny voices.
"Not far from here are two
strange green creatures," one
of the seahorses explained.
"They have flappy
black feet."
"Flappy black feet!" the
others repeated.
"And they're guarding a
big, white pearl,"
another added.
"A BIG WHITE PEARL!"
shouted all the seahorses together.
"They were over there by a tall,
pointy rock, next to the coral
reef," one seahorse explained.
"Over there, over there!" chorused
the others.

"Thank you, friends," Shannon said with a smile. "Come on, girls."

She swam off quickly, and Kirsty and Rachel followed. They only paused to wave at the seahorses, who were bobbing up and down in a frenzy of excitement.

It didn't take long to find the rock the seahorses had mentioned. Cautiously, Shannon and the girls peeked out from behind it.

"There they are," Shannon whispered. "And there's the Moon Pearl!"

Two goblins were playing catch with a big, creamy-white pearl. Kirsty caught her breath in wonder. She watched the pearl shimmer in the turquoise water as the goblins tossed it back and forth.

"It's not fair!" One of the goblins moaned. "We're stuck down here, guarding the Moon Pearl while

everyone else is surfing."

"Yeah, two new guards were supposed to come and take over after half an

hour," the other grumbled. "But nobody showed up!"

Shannon grinned at Rachel and Kirsty. "There are only two of them," she whispered. "This is our chance to get the pearl. But how?"

Rachel thought for a moment. "Maybe we could sneak over to the goblins and grab the pearl when it's in midair," she

suggested. "Like a game of monkey-in-the-middle."

Kirsty nodded. "There's some coral and clumps of seaweed to hide behind," she said eagerly. "Let's give it a try."

The three of them swam silently to a boulder covered with colorful sea anemones. Then they slipped through the gap between two large pieces of coral and hid behind a bunch of seaweed. They were very close to the goblins now.

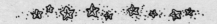

Anxiously, they all peered through the seaweed to see if the goblins had spotted them, but they were still tossing the pearl back and forth.

"OK, we're right between the goblins here," Shannon whispered. "Who's going to try to grab the pearl?"

"Rachel, you're good at ball games," said Kirsty.

"I'll give it a try," Rachel agreed bravely.

They all waited as one of the goblins prepared to throw the pearl back to the other.

"Now, Rachel!" Shannon said.

Rachel soared up from behind the seaweed at the same moment that the goblin tossed the pearl. As it flew

through the air, Rachel swam forward,
stretching out her arms to grab it.

Kirsty held her breath as she watched.
Would Rachel be able to reach the pearl
before the goblins realized what was
going on?

Seahorses Save the Day

Rachel felt her fingertips brush the surface of the pearl, but it was too high for her to catch. "Oh no!" She moaned as the pearl flew over her head.

"It's those pesky fairies!" yelled the goblin who had thrown the pearl.

With a determined look on his face, the other goblin zoomed through the water

with the help of his flippers. He snatched
the pearl before Rachel could try to grab
it again.

"Now, let's go!" the first goblin
shouted. "Hurry!"

The two goblins shot off through the
water, propelling themselves with their
huge magic flippers. Quickly, Shannon
and Kirsty joined Rachel.

"After them!" Shannon gasped.

The three girls swam swiftly after the goblins.

They raced along the coral reef, passing schools of fish and a very

surprised-looking turtle. But the
goblins, with the help of their
magic flippers, were just too
fast to catch.

"It's no use." Shannon panted as the goblins disappeared from sight. "They're too fast." She stopped and looked at Rachel and Kirsty in dismay. "How are we ever going to get the Moon Pearl back?" Suddenly, they heard a chorus of tiny voices say, "We can help! We can help!" The little seahorses were back, bobbing through the water in a long line. "Let us help you catch the goblins!"

"You can ride on our backs," one suggested.

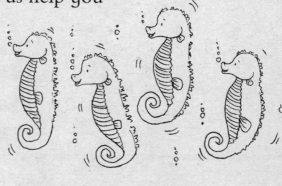

"You can ride on our backs!" the others agreed.

Shannon smiled. "That's very nice of you," she said gently, "but I don't think you'll be fast enough."

"We will, we will," the seahorses chorused. "We've been practicing. Now we're extra-fast!"

Shannon turned to Rachel and Kirsty.

"In that case, climb aboard!" she said, laughing.

Rachel and Kirsty each jumped onto
the back of a seahorse, and Shannon
did the same.

"Hold on! Hold tight!" the seahorses
shouted as they zoomed off.

"They *are* fast!" Kirsty gasped, clinging
to her seahorse's neck as they shot
through the water.

The seahorses were graceful, dodging
neatly around rocks and shells, and
racing in and out of coral arches.

"There are the goblins," Rachel said, as she caught a glimpse of them swimming ahead. "We're catching up to them!"

But how are we ever going to get the pearl away from them? Kirsty wondered as the seahorses whizzed past a clump of feathery seaweed. As she glanced at the long fronds waving in the water, she had an idea. "Maybe we could tie the goblins up with seaweed!"

"Good idea!" Shannon cried. She immediately raised her wand. With a burst of fairy magic, she knotted together some long strands of seaweed.

"Rachel, you take one end of the seaweed rope," Shannon instructed. "If your seahorse stays still when we get near the goblins, Kirsty and I can tie the goblins up."

"Stay still, stay still," Rachel's seahorse repeated, nodding his little head.

Quietly, Rachel, Kirsty, Shannon, and the seahorses snuck up behind the goblins.

"Now, everyone except Rachel and her seahorse, swim around the goblins as fast as you can," Shannon whispered.

The seahorses darted forward, except for Rachel's, who stayed very still. Rachel hung on to one end of the

seaweed rope, while Kirsty and Shannon held the rest of it.

"Hooray!" the seahorses yelled excitedly as they swam around the goblins. "Around and around and around we go!"

The Tide Turns

The goblins' eyes almost popped out of
their heads when they saw Kirsty,
Shannon, and the seahorses racing
around them.

"It's those fairies again!" one of them
yelled. "Let's get out of here!"

But before they could move, the
seaweed rope tightened, stopping them in

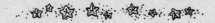

their tracks. The goblins cried out with
rage as the seaweed rope tied them up in
knots.

"Help!" the goblins shrieked.

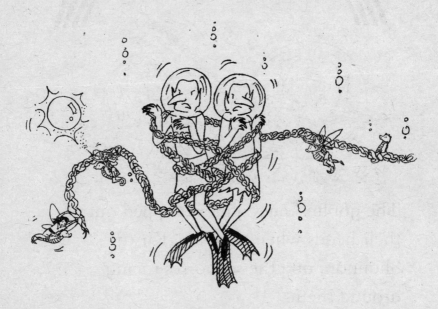

Rachel, Kirsty, and Shannon rode
their seahorses over to the goblins and
took the Moon Pearl right out of their
hands. The goblins scowled at them.

"When we let go of the rope, it will take you a little while to get free," Shannon told them. "That will give you time to think about what you've done."

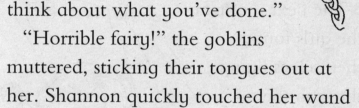

"Horrible fairy!" the goblins muttered, sticking their tongues out at her. Shannon quickly touched her wand

to the creamy surface of the Moon Pearl, and it instantly shrank to its Fairyland size. "Thank you, my friends," Shannon called to the

seahorses, who were still dancing
happily around the goblins. She waved
her wand, showering herself, Rachel,
and Kirsty with sparkles. "See you
again soon!"

"Bye-bye! Bye-bye!" the
seahorses called happily.

The next moment,
the girls found
themselves flying
through the air
as Shannon's
magic
whisked
them up
and out of
the sea.

"I think
the goblins

will rush back to Jack Frost to tell him they lost the Moon Pearl," Shannon called to Rachel and Kirsty. "Hopefully they'll leave Hawaii before any humans spot them." She glanced down and pointed with her wand. "Look, girls!"

Rachel and Kirsty saw that they were now flying over Fairyland. Rachel gasped. "Look at the river!" she cried. The twisting river that wound its way through the green fairy meadows had burst its banks. Lots of the toadstool houses were already surrounded by water!

"Fairyland is affected even more than the human world, because everything's so small," Shannon said.

Kirsty and Rachel were upset

E

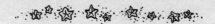

to see that the pink-and-white
Fairyland palace was also flooded.
Shannon swooped in through
the window of the Royal
Observatory, with the girls
right behind her.

Inside, they found King Oberon,
Queen Titania, and Cedric the Royal
Astronomer.

"Ah, we knew you wouldn't let us
down," King Oberon declared with a
smile as Shannon handed
the Moon Pearl to
Cedric.

Cedric
beamed as
he hurried
over to the
crystal box.
He placed the
Moon Pearl next to the
Dawn and Twilight Pearls, and all three
shimmered with a magical glow.

"Come and look out the window,
girls," said Queen Titania.

Kirsty and Rachel ran to see.

"The water level is going down already!" Kirsty cried, relieved.

They all watched happily as fairies began popping out of their little toadstool houses, cheering and clapping.

"This calls for a celebration!" Queen Titania proclaimed. "And what better way to celebrate than to finish our luau?"

Shannon and the girls glanced at each other in delight as the queen hurried off to organize the party.

Soon the luau was in full swing on the beach again. Kirsty, Rachel, and all the fairies joined in the singing and dancing.

"This is the best party ever!" Rachel sighed happily as the sun began to set on Fairyland.

Just then, King Oberon called for attention. "We want to thank Shannon the Ocean Fairy, and Rachel and Kirsty for saving Fairyland from flooding," he announced. "Without them, Jack Frost would still have our precious pearls."

The queen pointed her wand at Rachel and Kirsty, and a shower of fairy dust scattered around them. When it cleared, the girls gasped with delight.

They were each wearing a beautiful
gold ring with a rosy pink pearl on it that
looked just like the Dawn Pearl.

"Thank you," Rachel and Kirsty both
said gratefully.

"And now you should be getting home,"
said the queen, smiling widely at them.

Shannon gave the girls a big hug.
"Good-bye," she cried.

"Good-bye!" Rachel and Kirsty called,
waving to all their friends as the queen's
magic sent them flying home.

A few seconds later, the girls found themselves on the beach near Gran's house, back to their normal size again.

"Wasn't that an amazing adventure?" Kirsty said happily as they went up the cliff steps toward the house.

"Oh, yes," Rachel agreed, admiring her beautiful ring. "Our fairy adventures are always amazing. But this one under the sea was *extra* special!"

SPECIAL EDITION

Don't miss Rachel and Kirsty's
other summertime adventures!
Join them for beachy fun in

Joy
the Summer Vacation
Fairy!

Take a look at this special sneak peek. . . .

The Fairy Footprint

"Have you finished packing yet,
Rachel?" Mrs. Walker called up the
stairs. "Kirsty and her parents will be
here soon."

"Almost done!" Rachel Walker
shouted back. It was the beginning of
summer vacation and, in just a few
hours, she and her parents would be back

on Rainspell Island! Even better, Kirsty Tate, Rachel's best friend, was going to be staying there with her parents, too. The two girls had met on that same island the summer before. It had been a magical time!

Rachel only had two things left to pack — her toothbrush and her favorite T-shirt. She hunted through her drawers. Where was it? Just then, she glimpsed the corner of a sleeve sticking out from under her bed.

"Oh no!" she groaned, pulling the shirt out. There was a big ketchup stain on the front.

Upset that she hadn't asked her mom to wash it earlier, Rachel went to her bathroom to get her toothbrush.

When she came back, she gasped. The T-shirt was neatly folded on the bed, and the big stain had nearly disappeared! There was just one little mark on the sleeve.

Rachel leaned in to take a closer look. It wasn't just a mark. It was . . . a tiny, sandy footprint!

A ray of sunshine shone through the window, and the sleeve of her T-shirt glowed.

"Fairy dust!" Rachel breathed.

RAINBOW magic™

There's Magic in Every Series!

The Rainbow Fairies

The Weather Fairies

The Jewel Fairies

The Pet Fairies

The Fun Day Fairies

The Petal Fairies

The Dance Fairies

The Music Fairies

The Sports Fairies

The Party Fairies

The Ocean Fairies

Read them all!

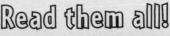

www.scholastic.com

www.rainbowmagiconline.com

HIT entertainment

RMFAIRY3